CHIEF
MINISTER

JT BALDWIN

"I have always believed that the measures we take today ensure the safety of tomorrow. Every difficult decision, every necessary sacrifice, every moment of moral compromise—all in service of a greater good that perhaps only I could see clearly. History may judge me harshly, but history has never borne the weight of protecting an entire continent from the chaos of unchecked freedom."

— From the private files of Chief Minister Shori Ashford, recovered after her fall from power

Series Guide | THE PALISADE JOURNALS

RECOMMENDED READING ORDER:

Vol. I — The Thermecine Road (2178)
Vol. II — Chief Minister (2191)
Vol. III — I, Marked (2173)
Vol. IV — Test of Character (2183)
Vol. V — Fortune Forged (2189)

CHRONOLOGICAL TIMELINE:

• 2173 | *I, Marked*
A girl named Anne becomes a weapon called Snips.

• 2178 | *The Thermecine Road*
Regal Eldain begins his descent down the road of vengeance.

• 2183 | *Test of Character*
Victoria Colwell witnesses an unspeakable transfer of power.

• 2189 | *Fortune Forged*
Peri Blackwood's first con and the cost of leadership.

▶ **2191 | *Chief Minister* ◀ You Are Here**
The highest office is not enough for Shori Ashford.

PART ONE

THE SUMMIT

Late Winter, 2191

Valdris Promontory | CAD Hamilton, Continental Authority

— ❖ —

Shori Ashford's heels struck the marble floors of Valdris Promontory, the imposing government complex that served as the seat of Continental Authority in CAD Hamilton. Each step was a declaration of authority echoing through corridors where morning light poured through towering windows, casting geometric shadows across floors worn smooth by thirty years of ministerial procession. To her left, the Valdris Sea stretched endlessly beyond floor-to-ceiling glass, while brass fixtures caught the light like captured sunlight, vaulted ceilings soaring forty feet above with stone arches carved in mathematical precision.

This was civilization when properly funded and ruthlessly maintained. While the world beyond staggered beneath failing infrastructure, the capital endured: pristine, unyielding, a testament to focused will.

Behind her, Elan Trevare's footsteps followed in perfect synchronization. One step behind. Always one step behind. His dark suit was immaculate, his posture composed, rose-tinted spectacles lending him an air of polite detachment. To casual observers, he was simply the Chief Minister's exceptionally competent assistant.

Shori had seen how conversations slowed when Elan entered a room, how colleagues' eyes followed his movements with wary respect. He understood that silence was its own form of control, a lesson she'd taught him well.

"Minister Ashford," came a voice from the left. Audra Nayel approached with measured steps, leather folio clutched against her chest. Fifty-something, steel-gray hair pulled into a severe bun, she carried herself with the weary dignity of someone who had briefed three Chief Ministers and watched each make the same mistakes in different clothes.

"Audra," Shori acknowledged without slowing. The older woman fell into step beside her, practiced in the art of walking briefings.

"Three governors have escalated their dissent. Margos, Kiron, and Western Territory. All requesting additional autonomy over internal resource allocation."

"They mistake survival for rebellion," Shori replied, her voice carrying just enough to reach the handful of aides and security personnel flanking their procession. "Remind them who feeds their cities."

A flicker passed through Audra's expression, not disagreement, but the particular fatigue of delivering unwelcome truths to those who preferred comfortable lies. "Of course, Minister. Though I should note that Governor Hale from Western Territory has specific concerns about recent federal resource extractions."

Shori's step never faltered, but something shifted in the air around them. She could sense Elan's attention focusing behind her, though he remained silent, tracking the faces of those they passed.

"I don't need to remind you that federal extraction operations fall under Continental Authority oversight," Shori said. "Governor Hale would do well to remember the distinction between his authority and mine."

They reached the intersection where the ministerial corridor branched toward the Council chambers. Here, Shori paused, not from uncertainty, but with calculated timing that understood even hesitation could be a tool.

"Anything else, Audra?"

"The morning's intelligence brief." The older woman produced a sealed envelope from the folio. "Agent Cassian's report from the Western Territory. He marked it immediate."

Shori accepted the envelope, noting its weight, the quality of the seal. Her field operative rarely marked reports immediate unless trouble was brewing beyond usual territorial unrest. "Thank you. That will be all."

Audra nodded and peeled away, disappearing into the bureaucratic maze of lesser corridors. Shori continued toward the chambers, Elan maintaining his silent accompaniment.

As they neared the Council chambers, polished silence gave way to chaos: raised voices, the sharp crack of a gavel failing to restore order, the shuffle of papers and urgent whispers that meant someone had lost control of the room. Shori's pace never faltered, but her eyes sharpened as they approached.

The double doors of dark wood and brass stood partially open, flanked by Continental Authority guards in formal black uniforms with crisp white trim. Ceremonial, but no less lethal for their polish. Through the gap, she could see ministers gesticulating wildly, aides scurrying between the crescent-shaped table and gallery behind it, papers scattered like autumn leaves.

But it wasn't the chaos that made Shori pause just shy of the threshold.

A figure in the gallery caught her attention: a young man, maybe twenty-five, leaning too far forward over the rail. His eyes gleamed with the intensity of someone recording rather than observing. His jacket hung awkwardly, the fit distorted by something underneath. His focus was too precise. Too hungry.

A journalist. Somehow, impossibly, a journalist had slipped past their screening protocols.

Shori's jaw tightened imperceptibly. She leaned toward Elan, her voice pitched low enough not to carry.

"Gallery. Third row, far left. Blue jacket, very last season and awful fit. He doesn't belong."

Elan's gaze flicked across the chamber, locking onto the target in seconds. "Shall I have security handle it?"

"No. Too public. Handle it quietly. Make it instructive."

Elan nodded once, something dark flickering behind his rose-tinted spectacles. "Of course, Minister."

She broke the seal on Cassian's envelope, scanning the brief contents while Elan melted away into the bureaucratic maze. Three lines. Code words. A location. And at the bottom, a single word that sent ice through her veins: *Confirmed.*

The Western Territory situation was escalating faster than anticipated. Her most sensitive operations were at risk of exposure. All the more reason to clean house here first.

Shori straightened, slipping the message into her jacket's inner pocket. Through the doorway, the argument was reaching fever pitch: something about resource allocation, territorial disputes, the usual provincial squabbling that threatened to tear the continent apart if left unchecked.

They needed guidance. They needed control.

They needed her.

She stepped through the threshold, and the effect was instantaneous. The chamber's temperature seemed to drop as conversations died mid-sentence. Chairs scraped against marble as ministers rose from their seats around the great crescent table. Even the aides in the gallery fell silent, pressing back against the walls like startled birds.

"The Chief Minister of the Continental Authority," announced Captain Vaelen Jor, his voice carrying the practiced authority of someone who had called this room to order a thousand times. "The Honorable Shori Ashford."

The chamber was magnificent, built to inspire both awe and submission. The crescent table dominated the floor, polished mahogany that could seat twenty but currently held twelve of the continent's most powerful individuals. Behind them, the gallery provided space for their assistants and advisors, partially screened to maintain the illusion of intimate governance while allowing for necessary support.

But it was the far wall that truly commanded attention: floor-to-ceiling windows overlooking the Valdris Sea, where morning light danced across waves stretching to the eastern horizon. The view served as both inspiration and reminder. This was the edge of their world, the boundary between order and chaos.

Shori began her walk down the central aisle with measured pace. CA guards stood at perfect attention at every entry point, their black and white uniforms lending gravity to the proceedings.

As she moved, her eyes swept the room, cataloguing faces, reading expressions, noting who met her gaze and who looked away. Minister Korvyn stood straighter as she passed. Councilman Thorne's hand twitched toward papers he clearly wished he could hide. And there, fourth seat from the left, Minister Kaine of Internal Affairs watched with dark hair framing sharp eyes, her gaze carrying the perfect balance of respect and challenge.

The chaos of moments before seemed impossible now. This was how it should be: ordered, respectful, controlled. She was not the enemy of these people's ambitions. She was the architect of a system that allowed those ambitions to flourish within proper boundaries.

The Seat waited at the head of the crescent, not quite a throne but elevated enough to command the room, positioned so she could see every face while the Valdris Sea provided a backdrop of endless possibility.

Shori reached her chair and remained standing, allowing the moment to stretch. In the silence, she could hear the distant crash of waves against cliffs below, the faint hum of the building's life support systems, the careful breathing of twelve individuals who held the fate of millions in their hands.

This was leadership. Not the petty squabbling and shortsightedness that had nearly torn them apart before, but a unified vision, disciplined, deliberate, and necessary.

All of it, resting, inevitably, in her hands.

"Please," she said, her voice carrying easily to every corner of the chamber, "be seated."

As chairs scraped against marble and papers rustled, Shori settled into her seat, leather sighing softly beneath her. Her gaze found familiar faces around the crescent table: Minister Korvyn, solid and dependable; Councilman Thorne, whose nervous energy always betrayed whatever scheme he was hatching; Minister Kaine, whose dark eyes held something that looked like patient calculation.

"Minister," Shori acknowledged Vanessa Kaine with a slight nod.

"Chief," came the reply, delivered with crisp professionalism that revealed nothing while somehow managing to suggest everything.

"I trust we can proceed with today's agenda in a more orderly fashion than when I arrived?"

A murmur of agreement rippled around the table. Minister Dacian, a man whose jowls seemed to grow more prominent with each passing session, cleared his throat and gestured to the stack of papers before him.

"If I may, Chief Minister, we were discussing the Southern Infrastructure Revitalization Act. Specifically, the proposal to rebuild rail lines past Bethshelm to serve the overlooked communities of our southwestern territories."

Shori accepted the briefing packet from an aide, scanning the executive summary. The language was flowery enough: promises to "bring these forgotten regions into the full standing and prosperity of the Continental Authority," commitments to "infrastructure equality" and "economic justice."

The reality, as always, was more complex.

"Minister Dacian," she said, not looking up from the document, "how many rail lines currently service the southwestern region, and how many does this act actually address?"

Dacian's jowls quivered as he shuffled papers. "Forty-three active lines, Chief Minister, but their condition varies significantly. The focus is on establishing a flagship route that will demonstrate our commitment..."

"One." Shori set the packet down with deliberate precision, silver-gray eyes pinning him. "This bill allocates seventeen billion holdings to rebuild one rail line while the other forty-two continue to deteriorate." She flipped to page twelve, where the real meat of the legislation lived. "Meanwhile, section four grants no-bid contracts to Meridian Development, section seven hands mineral rights to Kavron Mining, and section nine..." She looked up. "Section nine is luxury resort subsidies disguised as infrastructure."

The chamber fell silent. The held breath of those who had been caught.

"The southwestern territories deserve better than political theater," Shori continued, her voice carrying just enough edge to cut. "They deserve actual infrastructure, not monuments to our friends' bank accounts disguised as charity."

Minister Graylen, the Continental Treasurer, leaned forward with visible agitation. His face had taken on the mottled red of a man unaccustomed to having his financial arrangements questioned in public.

"Chief Minister, with respect, the fiscal realities of reconstruction require private partnership. These contracts ensure rapid deployment of resources..."

"These contracts ensure your campaign contributors receive no-bid windfalls while families in Kavron still lack reliable power." Shori's tone remained level, but something sharp flickered behind her words. "The Continental Authority's credibility cannot survive another 'reconstruction' that reconstructs only the net worth of those who already have enough."

She stood, the motion drawing every eye in the room. "I propose we table this legislation pending a full audit of existing southwestern infrastructure needs. Real needs, not imagined opportunities. When we rebuild, we rebuild right."

Minister Kaine spoke into the resulting silence, her voice carefully neutral. "A prudent approach, Chief. Perhaps we might also consider involving local representatives in the planning process?"

There it was: support wrapped in suggestion, offering Shori a graceful path while subtly implying oversight might be needed. The dance of politics made visible.

"An excellent point, Minister. Transparency serves everyone's interests."

Graylen's pen scratched furiously across his notepad, calculating how many favors he'd have to call in to resurrect his pet project. Useful for his financial acumen, but his inability to see beyond the next quarterly report made him predictable. Profitable corruption was still corruption.

Shori settled back into her chair, satisfied. The Continental Authority would not become a feeding trough for the wealthy. The greater good required difficult choices, some so terrible they kept her awake nights, but those choices had to serve something larger than personal enrichment.

"Shall we move to the next item?"

Minister Korvyn consulted his agenda. "Agricultural Relief Initiative for the Northbridge District. Emergency water assistance following the seasonal drought."

Shori accepted another briefing packet, though she barely glanced at it. Northbridge: a small farming community along the narrow land corridor connecting the Continental Authority to the larger Freehold territories. Officially, they were experiencing drinking water shortages due to unusually dry conditions. Officially, the Continental Authority was responding with humanitarian aid and agricultural support.

Officially.

"The request is for immediate deployment of hydration specialists and soil assessment teams," Korvyn continued. "Estimated duration of six to eight weeks, pending environmental recovery."

Shori set the packet aside. Six to eight weeks would be more than enough time for her people to map the corridor's defensive positions, identify potential sympathizers among the local population, and establish infrastructure needed for future diplomatic initiatives.

"This matter hardly requires Council deliberation," she said, her voice carrying the faint impatience of someone forced to waste time on obvious decisions. "People are thirsty. We provide water. I'm invoking Administrative Rule Forty-Seven. Emergency humanitarian aid falls under executive authority."

Minister Graylen, still smarting from the infrastructure defeat, seized the opportunity to reassert influence. "Chief Minister, while I appreciate the urgency, shouldn't we at least discuss the budgetary implications? These deployment costs..."

"Are negligible compared to the moral cost of allowing our neighbors to suffer while we debate procedure. Unless you're suggesting we abandon our humanitarian principles for the sake of bookkeeping?"

The trap was perfectly laid. No one could argue against helping drought-stricken farmers without appearing callous. The room fell silent except for the scratch of a pen as someone noted the decision in the official record.

"The motion is approved. Minister Korvyn, coordinate with the Agricultural Department for immediate deployment."

As Shori spoke, she caught Elan slipping back into the chamber, adjusting his cuffs with the same precision he'd used for everything else that morning. His subtle nod confirmed the journalist was no longer a problem. Efficient, as always.

The real deployment orders were already prepared, waiting in a sealed envelope that would find its way to very different hands than the Agricultural Department. Sometimes the most important work happened in the spaces between words, in humanitarian gestures that served multiple masters. The farmers of Northbridge would indeed receive aid, enough to maintain the fiction, enough to keep them grateful.

And in return, the Continental Authority would gain something far more valuable than their loyalty.

Information.

"Any other business?" Shori asked, already reaching for her papers to signal the session's end.

Minister Kaine raised her hand with deliberate precision. "If I may, Chief."

Shori's fingers paused on the documents. "Minister."

"I've received concerning reports about labor unrest in our eastern manufacturing districts. The steel mill strikes in Bethshelm and North York have left nearly three thousand workers without income for six weeks now." Her voice carried the careful neutrality of someone delivering facts, but there was something underneath, a sharpness that suggested deeper knowledge. "These are skilled positions, Chief. The kind of expertise we can't afford to lose to alternative employment opportunities."

Alternative employment. Such a delicate way to reference problems Shori preferred to handle quietly.

"The Labor Relations Department is addressing the situation," Shori replied evenly. "Union negotiations are proceeding within normal parameters."

"Of course. Though I wonder if we might consider more direct intervention. These workers have families, mortgages, obligations that don't pause for contract disputes." A slight pause, perfectly timed. "Desperate people make regrettable choices."

The implication hung in the air. Everyone in the room heard concern for workers. Shori heard something else entirely.

"Your concern for their welfare is noted," Shori said, her tone cooling by degrees. "I'm certain the appropriate departments will find suitable guidance for anyone considering poor decisions."

Their eyes met across the chamber. For a heartbeat, the formal mask slipped on both sides, just enough to acknowledge that this conversation had multiple layers, that both women understood far more than they were saying.

"Of course, Chief. Guidance is always preferable to correction."

◇

The session concluded with usual procedural formalities. But Shori remained seated, watching as the chamber slowly emptied.

As the ministers filed out, their murmurs fading, Shori lingered at the Seat, watching Minister Kaine gather her materials with unhurried precision. When the last of the other council members had departed, Nessa approached with the same measured steps she'd used to deliver her veiled challenge.

"Chief," she said quietly, stopping just within conversational range.

"Walk with me," Shori replied, rising from her chair. Not a request.

They moved toward the chamber's side exit, their footsteps echoing in the vast space. Behind them, Elan followed at his customary distance, close enough to intervene, far enough to maintain the illusion of privacy.

"You seem energetic today," Shori observed as they reached the corridor beyond the chamber doors. "Eager to contribute to our deliberations."

"I serve at the Council's pleasure, Chief. When I see opportunities to be useful..."

"Useful." Shori stopped walking, turning to face the other woman fully. "Such an interesting word choice. Almost as interesting as your sudden expertise in metallurgical labor relations."

For a moment, something flickered behind the professional mask, a spark of the person Shori remembered from years past, when their conversations had taken place in very different settings.

"I've always been observant," came the careful reply. "You used to appreciate that quality."

"I appreciated many of your qualities." Shori's voice dropped lower, intimate in the way that spoke of shared history. "I remember how gracefully you moved when we danced at Fort Delvaine. That careful waltz in the officers' lounge. The way you followed my lead so perfectly."

Color rose in the other woman's cheeks, but her composure never wavered. "Those were different times, Chief."

"Indeed they were." Shori stepped closer, her voice becoming silk wrapped around steel. "Times when you knew your place in the music. When you followed my lead instead of trying to change the tempo."

The warning was clear, delivered with the kind of gentle precision that made it all the more threatening.

"I haven't forgotten the steps," came the quiet response. "But perhaps the song has changed."

They stood there for a moment, two women who had once shared secrets and soft touches, now separated by power and suspicion and choices that couldn't be undone. The marble halls stretched around them, empty except for the distant echo of their breathing.

"I trust it won't change too dramatically," Shori said finally. "Some dances require traditional choreography."

Without waiting for a response, she turned and began walking toward her private offices. Elan fell into step behind her, silent as always, but she could feel his attention focused on the woman they left standing in the corridor.

"Elevate her," Shori said quietly, not turning back.

"Chief?"

"Put her on your watch list. She's pushing her luck."

"Of course, Minister."

She would need to be reminded of the boundaries. Gently, at first.

The marble floors echoed their purpose as they made their way toward the private chambers where real decisions were made, where masks could be set aside, and where assets like Aerin Revalis waited for orders that would shape the continent's hidden future.

CHIEF MINISTER

PART TWO

ASSIGNMENT

Early Spring, 2191

Sub-Level Three, CAD Hamilton

— ❖ —

Shortly after the successful session, Shori Ashford descended the long staircase that connected the upper government floors to her private offices three stories beneath CAD Hamilton's marble grandeur. The wide steps, reminiscent of the grand medical complexes from before the Collapse, provided both practical access and psychological separation, a deliberate transition from the theater of public governance to the reality of necessary decisions.

Captain Vaelen Jor led their small procession, his imposing frame clearing the path with polite but unmistakable authority. Staff members stepped aside with respectful nods, conversations pausing until the Chief

Minister had passed. Behind her, two guards maintained professional distance, close enough to respond to threats, far enough to preserve the illusion of accessibility.

"How is your family, Elan?" Shori asked, her voice carrying easily in the stairwell's acoustic space.

"They are well, ma'am," came the reply from beside her, delivered with the same measured neutrality he brought to all personal inquiries.

Perfectly professional. Completely uninformative. Elan Trevare's personal life remained as efficiently compartmentalized as his administrative duties.

They reached the security checkpoint at Sub-Level Three, where two additional guards snapped to attention before resuming their posts. The heavy doors beyond opened into a circular foyer that served as the heart of Shori's private administrative complex. Reinforced concrete walls replaced the ornamental stone of the upper levels, and the only decoration was a single oil painting, a pre-collapse landscape of rolling hills under an endless sky, the kind of world that existed now only in memory and aspiration.

"Chief Minister!" Dani Castell looked up from her desk with the bright attention of someone still discovering the weight of important work. At twenty-two, she carried herself with the poise expected of someone whose uncle served on the Agricultural Council, though her enthusiasm remained refreshingly genuine. She rose quickly, files clutched against her chest.

"Dani." Shori replied with warmth that came naturally. "I trust the afternoon treated you well?"

"Very well, thank you, Chief Minister. Your guests have arrived. Dr. Baeriss and Agent Revalis are waiting in the reception area."

"Excellent timing." Shori glanced around the foyer's familiar layout. Dani's desk commanded a clear view of the entrance, while discreet doors provided access to the various functions of her private complex: Jor's security station and extended staff offices to the left, her private consultation chamber to the right.

"Captain Jor, if you would retrieve our guests?"

"Of course, Chief Minister," Jor replied, his bearing shifting subtly from protective escort to ceremonial function.

As he moved toward the reception area, Shori felt the familiar transition from public leadership to the more complex work that happened in spaces designed for difficult conversations. Here, three stories beneath the marble grandeur where democracy performed its careful theater, the real business of continental governance took place.

The work that others couldn't understand. The work that someone had to do.

Shori entered her private consultation chamber. A steel desk dominated the room, its surface bearing a mechanical chronometer, a gift from Pence Garda during her early years, that ticked with precise rhythm. Beside it, a delicate crystal paperweight held down classified documents, its faceted surface catching and fracturing the overhead light into rainbow fragments.

But it was the terminal that truly captured attention. Built into the desk's surface, its brownish translucent glass housing gleamed like amber in the overhead lighting, while three vacuum tubes of varying sizes glowed softly behind the screen. As the system processed encrypted communications, the tubes pulsed with gentle warmth, accompanied by the subtle electronic sounds of analog technology warming to its purpose. Green lettering scrolled across the brown-tinted display, routing schedules for the Western Territory that masked far more sensitive logistics.

Minutes later, she heard Jor's announcement from the foyer: "Chief Minister, Dr. Evelyn Baeriss and Agent Aerin Revalis."

"Send them in, Captain."

The heavy doors swung open on well-oiled hinges. Captain Jor stepped aside with military precision, his heroic bearing, square jaw, piercing blue eyes, and that small scar along his left cheekbone that spoke of real combat, a stark contrast to the utilitarian surroundings.

Dr. Evelyn Baeriss entered with the same mechanical efficiency she'd displayed since her teenage years, though thirty-four had refined her restless energy into something approaching artistry. Her lab coat was pristine, dark hair pulled back with a clip of her own design. Round glasses reflected the terminal's glow as her dark eyes immediately began a systematic assessment of the room's systems.

Aerin Revalis followed with fluid grace, her enhanced physiology evident in every controlled movement. Twenty-six years old, just under six feet of lean muscle and perfect balance. Her black hair was braided tight with silver wire threading, not decorative, but functional channels for her enhanced abilities. Her mahogany skin carried subtle scars from the enhancement process, thin lines along her throat and wrists where Ro'Daerim steel nodes had been integrated. Golden-amber eyes swept the room with predatory awareness, cataloguing exits, weapons, threats with the automatic assessment of someone trained to survive impossible odds.

Behind them, Elan followed at his customary distance, clipboard in hand.

Aerin moved past the entrance, offering Jor a professional nod as she passed. "Captain."

"Agent Revalis," he replied with respectful acknowledgment, stepping aside to allow her passage.

Captain Jor's frame vanished behind the closing double doors.

"Chief Minister," Evelyn acknowledged while moving to her seat, though her attention had already drifted to the terminal's amber glow. "The vacuum tube array. Fascinating adaptation of pre-collapse technology. The harmonic resonance patterns suggest significant processing capability."

"Dr. Baeriss. Agent Revalis. Please, be seated."

Aerin took the chair that provided the clearest view of both doors. Evelyn settled near the terminal, her eyes continuing their mechanical assessment.

"Before we begin," Shori said, "how is Taegus progressing? I know the recovery has been... challenging."

Evelyn looked up from her notebook, her expression shifting to clinical optimism. "He's responding well to the latest treatments, showing measurable progress. The integration processes have required adjustment, but the results are encouraging."

"That's good. I do miss him. Give him my best when you see him next."

"Of course, Chief Minister."

The brief exchange satisfied the courtesies while avoiding deeper discussion. Some recoveries required methods better left unexamined.

"We have a situation that requires immediate attention," she began, activating a privacy field that created a subtle hum in the air around them. "Intelligence has identified a resource in the Western Territory that could significantly enhance our program capabilities."

She opened a classified folder, revealing a series of photographs taken with telephoto lenses. The images showed a family compound in the Western Territory, modest buildings clustered around a central courtyard, with what appeared to be a metalworking shop and small residential structures. But it was the people that drew attention: a family of four, including a teenage girl whose eyes caught the light with a metallic sheen that didn't belong to any normal iris color.

"Western Territory, approximately three hundred kilometers northwest of Millhaven," Shori explained, spreading the photographs across her desk with clinical precision. "Small settlement, mostly agricultural with some specialty metalworking. Standard frontier community, unremarkable except for this."

She indicated the girl in the photographs. Perhaps fifteen years old, with long dark hair and the unmistakable rust-colored irises, carrying that distinctive metallic reflection, that marked high Ferric blood resonance.

"Her name is Isamuko Eli," Shori continued. "Parents operate a blacksmith and mechanical repair shop, which explains the advanced metalworking capabilities in the area. But more importantly, preliminary assessment suggests she represents one of the highest natural Ferric counts we've encountered outside our existing program."

Evelyn leaned forward, studying the photographs with focused intensity. "Ferric resonance levels?"

"Initial estimates suggest she exceeds baseline thresholds by a factor of three. If accurate, her blood compatibility would provide sufficient material for multiple enhancement procedures over an extended period."

Evelyn's stylus paused over her notebook. "These numbers exceed even the Pinecrest subject from my early assessments. I'd estimate her compatibility index is thirty percent higher than our previous record holder."

Something shifted in Shori's expression. A flicker of recognition that carried weight beyond professional interest. "The Pinecrest readings were exceptional. But that subject was extracted at optimal age for processing. This candidate's maturation presents different challenges, though not insurmountable ones."

"Timeline?" Aerin asked quietly.

"Soon. The settlement is entering its quieter season. Fewer travelers, reduced trade activity, minimal outside observation. The family maintains predictable routines that provide optimal acquisition opportunities."

"Resistance capability?" Aerin's question carried the weight of experience with operations that had faced complications.

"Minimal. Frontier self-reliance, some hunting weapons, but no organized security infrastructure. The population is spread thin across a wide area. Individual resistance is possible, but coordinated response would require significant organization time."

"Complications?" Evelyn asked, making notes.

"Secondary objectives. The family has developed techniques for working with specialty materials that could have applications for our program. We'll want to acquire technical assets along with the primary resource."

Shori set down a final photograph showing the girl working alongside her father in the metalworking shop, rust-colored eyes focused on some intricate task that required both precision and inherited skill.

"The mission is straightforward," she said, collecting the photographs and sliding them back into the folder. "Proceed to the Western Territory under agricultural aid cover. Locate and secure the identified resource. Documentation will reflect civilian agricultural assessment work."

"Acquisition approach?" Aerin asked.

"Start with recruitment if circumstances allow, but resource security is the priority. Use whatever approach ensures success with minimal local complications."

"Transportation and communication?"

"Military transport to the regional hub, civilian documentation for local travel. Check in every seventy-two hours through established channels. Emergency extraction available if needed, though clean completion is preferable."

Shori closed the folder with quiet finality. "Questions?"

Aerin shook her head. "Parameters are clear, Chief Minister."

Evelyn looked up from her technical notes. "I'd recommend comprehensive baseline measurements once the resource is secured. Given the potential compatibility levels, we'll want detailed analysis before beginning any extraction procedures."

"Noted. After the asset is acquired, stop through the agency outside of the Morrison Transfer Station to verify baseline measurements. Agent Revalis, you depart tomorrow morning."

A soft chime from her desk chronometer indicated the session's conclusion. Shori rose with practiced grace. Reaching down, she pressed a well-worn button on her terminal. "Captain Jor," she called, her voice carrying enough authority to reach the foyer beyond with or without the intercom.

The heavy doors opened immediately, revealing Jor's imposing figure.

"Dr. Baeriss, Agent Revalis," Shori continued, moving around her desk with diplomatic bearing, "thank you for your dedication to this resource acquisition mission. The agricultural assessment work you'll be conducting represents exactly the kind of forward-thinking aid that distinguishes our administration's approach to territorial development."

She extended her hand to each woman in turn. Warmth and authority in equal measure.

As the consultation concluded, Shori turned to Dani, who had been waiting patiently in the foyer. "Before we finish for the day, run down to Treasury and get me the actual infrastructure numbers for the southwestern rail project. Minister Dacian's figures were... optimistic."

"Of course, Chief Minister," Dani replied, already reaching for her notepad.

"And stop by the cafeteria and grab us each a slice of that cake I smelled earlier. Tell Perry I'm ensuring it's good enough for everyone." Shori added with a conspiratorial wink.

Dani's face lit up with a genuine smile. "I'll make sure he knows it's for quality control purposes."

The chamber's amber lighting settled back into its normal rhythms. The vacuum tubes pulsed with gentle warmth. The chronometer maintained its precise rhythm.

Shori watched the amber light settle over her terminal and thought about the girl with rust-colored eyes in the metalworking shop. The assignment was straightforward. The cost of it was something she'd stopped calculating years ago.

PART THREE

The Interception

Mid Spring, 2191

Valdris Promontory, CAD Hamilton

— ❖ —

The morning intelligence summary was routine until it wasn't.

Shori worked through the stack with the practiced efficiency of someone who processed a continent's worth of information before lunch. Three territorial disputes requiring mediation. A budget overrun in the northern infrastructure program. An update on fishing subsidy negotiations that managed to be simultaneously urgent and meaningless.

Then the sealed envelope. Cassian's handwriting. Priority classification.

She broke the seal.

The report was brief. Field reports always were. Operatives learned early that brevity was both security and mercy. But what it lacked in length it compensated for in precision.

PRIORITY   SECURE   /   EYES   ONLY

FROM: Specialist Russell - Field Station 9a, Eastern Corridor
TO: Chief Minister S. Ashford
RE: Transit Operation — Subject 437-B

Transport intercepted. Day 2191.117, 06:20 local. Eastern rail corridor, between Graphton and Valcross Junction.

Asset lost during transit. Escort team incapacitated — five personnel, non-fatal injuries. Team leader (Sgt. Matthews) reports two unknowns. No organizational affiliation identified. No enhancement signatures detected.

Repeat: non-enhanced civilians.

Transport vehicle disabled. Communications equipment destroyed. Escort personnel restrained with their own equipment and left at the site.

Asset not recovered. Current location unknown.

Perimeter blockade established at 0827. No confirmed sightings as of this report.
Spc. Russell

Shori read it twice. The second time slower.

Five trained guards. Armed. Operating under protocol. Incapacitated by two civilians who then vanished with the most valuable extraction target her program had acquired in years.

Twenty days. She'd had her for twenty days. The girl had been in transit to the processing facility, baseline measurements confirmed, preliminary compatibility assessment exceeding every projection Evelyn had generated. A resource that represented years of strategic acquisition work, identified through Aerin's careful fieldwork in the Western Territory, extracted with minimal local disruption.

Gone.

Taken by people who, according to the field report, weren't even professionals.

She set the report on her desk. Aligned it with the edge. Precise. Controlled. The way she aligned everything when the alternative was breaking something.

"Elan."

He appeared in the doorway. He was always near when the tone of her voice changed.

"Get me Agent Revalis."

"She's currently debriefing from the Meridian assessment, Chief Minister. Shall I..."

"Now."

The word carried no volume. It didn't need to.

Elan departed. Shori stood and moved to the window. The Valdris Sea stretched to the horizon under a spring sky that had no interest in her operational setbacks. Fishing boats worked the water. Transport ships moved through regulated channels. The machinery of territorial commerce continuing its reliable rhythms while somewhere in the eastern corridor, a rust-eyed girl was being hidden by people who had no idea what they'd taken or what was coming for them.

Non-enhanced civilians. The phrase sat wrong. Not because it was inaccurate but because it was insufficient. Trained operatives failed for specific reasons: superior force, better intelligence, systemic compromise. Civilians succeeded through unpredictability. Through the particular recklessness of people who didn't understand the rules well enough to follow them.

That made them harder to anticipate. Not harder to find.

The door opened. Aerin entered with the controlled efficiency that characterized everything about her. Black braids. Silver wire threading. Amber eyes that found Shori's expression and read the situation before a word was spoken.

"We've lost the Eli girl," Shori said. No preamble. Aerin didn't require it.

Something shifted behind Aerin's amber gaze. Not surprise. Recalibration. The particular adjustment of someone who had already been working this problem from a different angle and was now incorporating new data.

"When?"

"Hours ago. Eastern corridor transit. Two unknowns intercepted. Non-enhanced. No organizational match."

"The escort?"

"Alive. Incapacitated. Five personnel who should have been adequate for a sedated minor in transit restraints." Shori handed her the field report. "Sergeant Matthews is requesting mobilization authority for a recovery operation."

Aerin read the report in the time it took Shori to return to her desk. "Matthews is competent but limited. Recovery requires different capabilities."

"Agreed. Which is why you're going." Shori settled into her chair. "I want the asset recovered. I want the interceptors identified. And I want to understand how two civilians defeated a trained escort team without enhancement signatures."

"Timeline?"

"Now."

Aerin folded the report with precise movements. "I'll need field authorization for the eastern corridor. Communication protocols. And discretion regarding the nature of the asset."

"You'll have everything you need." Shori paused. "Aerin. This girl represents the highest natural compatibility we've identified since the Pinecrest subject. Losing her isn't an option we can absorb."

"Understood, Chief Minister."

Aerin left the way she'd entered: controlled, silent, already calculating approach vectors and probability matrices for recovery operations that would begin within hours.

Shori sat in the silence that followed and thought about rust-colored eyes in a metalworking shop in the Western Territory. The girl who couldn't sit still. The sister who had too much spark for her own good.

Two civilians had taken her. Stolen her off a train with nothing but nerve and whatever crude capabilities passed for competence in the frontier territories.

Petty criminals. Opportunists. People who had stumbled into something they didn't understand and would soon discover the consequences of their ignorance.

She would have the girl back within the week.

✿

Aerin's reports arrived with mechanical regularity. Each one professionally comprehensive. Each one confirming the same essential fact: the interceptors had vanished into the eastern territories with an efficiency that suggested either extraordinary luck or a support network that didn't appear in any intelligence database.

The name arrived in Aerin's third report. A single entry, sourced from the escort team leader's debriefing.

Peri.

First name only. No surname match in any system Aerin could access. No organizational affiliation. No prior intelligence contact.

An unknown with copper hair who had defeated five trained guards and disappeared with the most valuable asset Shori's program had ever identified.

Shori filed the name alongside the operational setback and turned to more pressing matters. The Council session approaching. Nessa's investigations growing bolder. The political landscape requiring attention that a single lost asset, however valuable, couldn't justify monopolizing.

The frontier produced criminals the way it produced weeds: constantly, indiscriminately, and without lasting significance. This Peri would surface eventually. They always did.

And when she did, Aerin would be waiting.

PART FOUR

The Room Where it Happens

Late Summer, 2191

Solarium Suite, Ministerial Tower, CAD Hamilton

The Solarium Suite offered Shori a sweeping view of Hamilton's lights through its glass walls. By day, the space filled with sunlight regulated through mechanical shutters and prisms. By night, it became an observatory where the continent's most powerful could dine while surveying their domain.

Tonight, it awaited a more intimate gathering.

Shori stood near the eastern windows, watching traffic move through illuminated streets forty-three stories below. The city pulsed with ordered energy: transportation following prescribed routes, commerce flowing through regulated channels, citizens pursuing their lives within the boundaries of continental stability.

This was what she'd built. What she'd sacrificed everything to preserve.

Behind her, dinner had been arranged with characteristic precision. A mahogany table set for two, crystal glasses catching light from overhead fixtures, and a Vicester red breathing in a cut-glass decanter. Aged beef and root vegetables. Simple food, expertly prepared.

A soft chime announced the private elevator's arrival. Shori composed her expression, settling into the persona she would need for the evening ahead.

"Chief Minister," came the familiar voice, professionally neutral but carrying undertones of shared history.

"Nessa." Shori turned, offering a smile that felt both genuine and calculated. "Thank you for accepting the invitation."

Nessa Kaine stepped into the solarium with the confidence that belonged in such spaces. Two years as Minister of Internal Affairs had refined her natural authority, but something rougher remained beneath the polish, the woman who had once planned operations in field conditions rather than conference rooms. She wore a dark evening jacket over tailored trousers, hair pulled back in a style that managed to be both practical and elegant.

"Nice view," Nessa said, moving toward the western windows where the last light painted the horizon in gold and amber. "Good for keeping perspective on things."

Shori recognized the deliberate casualness. Nessa had never been comfortable with formal diplomatic language, preferring directness even when it cost her political points. Victoria must be working overtime trying to smooth those edges.

"Perspective helps," Shori agreed, joining her at the windows. "From this height, problems seem more manageable. Individual concerns become part of larger patterns."

"Assuming you're not too far up to see the real consequences."

There it was. The challenge delivered with Nessa's characteristic bluntness, wrapped in just enough civility to maintain pretense. Shori felt the careful equilibrium she'd planned shifting into something more dangerous.

"Shall we sit?" she suggested, gesturing toward the table. "The wine's been breathing, and we both know this conversation deserves better than small talk."

They settled into their chairs with the easy movements of two people who had shared countless meals in far less elegant circumstances. Shori poured wine while Nessa waited with the patience of someone who understood tactical timing.

"Vicester red," Shori noted, offering the glass. "I remembered your preference for Freehold vintages."

"You remember a lot of things." Nessa accepted the wine but didn't drink immediately. "Question is which ones you've decided to act on."

Shori took a sip, buying time while she processed the subtext. This wasn't going to be the careful diplomatic dance she'd hoped for. Nessa was playing her old game: direct pressure designed to force reactions rather than responses.

"How are you finding Internal Affairs?" Shori asked, trying to steer toward safer ground. "The position suits you better than I expected."

"You mean better than field work?" Nessa's smile carried genuine amusement. "Turns out hunting patterns in data isn't that different from hunting patterns in terrain. Same instincts, different tools."

"And what patterns have you been hunting lately?"

"Resource allocation irregularities. Personnel transfers that don't match official justifications. Communication networks designed to avoid oversight rather than facilitate it." Nessa paused, her gaze direct across the table. "The kind of patterns that suggest either massive incompetence or deliberate deception."

Shori carved beef with deliberate precision, using the action to mask her reaction. This was reconnaissance, not dinner conversation.

"Governance requires flexibility," she said carefully. "Official channels aren't always adequate for urgent situations. Adaptation is the difference between effective leadership and bureaucratic paralysis."

"And accountability?"

"Results speak louder than procedures."

"Tell that to the communities that pay the price for your flexibility."

The words carried the weight of personal knowledge rather than abstract moral concern. Shori set down her fork, recognizing that subtlety was no longer an option.

"You've changed," she said. "You once understood that difficult choices serve larger purposes. You helped plan operations that required comprehensive solutions."

"I helped plan operations I thought served legitimate security interests." Nessa's voice grew quieter, more intense. "Before I realized some of those operations had nothing to do with security and everything to do with systematic exploitation."

"Exploitation of what?"

"People. Communities. Children." Nessa leaned forward slightly. "You told me we weren't doing that anymore, Shori. The trafficking operations, the Andori partnerships. You said we'd moved beyond those methods."

Shori felt something cold settle in her stomach, but her voice remained steady. "Don't play the moral high ground with me, Nessa. You're just as guilty as I was back then. You helped plan those operations, you signed off on the protocols, you recruited assets for those networks. Your hands are every bit as bloody as mine."

"True." Nessa's diplomatic mask slipped completely. "But unlike you, I'm trying to undo my crimes. You're still justifying them."

"And what exactly do you think 'undoing' accomplishes?" Shori snapped. "The children are already processed. The operations already completed. Your guilt doesn't resurrect the dead or heal the broken."

"Maybe not. But it can stop more from being broken." Nessa's voice carried new intensity. "You want to talk about accountability? Let's talk about the Ossuary program. Let's talk about what happens to the families whose children disappear into your comprehensive solutions."

"Children who would otherwise be lost to circumstance or worse," Shori said. "Children who are given purpose, training, the opportunity to serve something greater than themselves."

"Children who are processed like raw materials." Nessa's voice turned harder. "You're harvesting them, Shori. Taking kids from their families and turning them into weapons."

"I'm protecting the continent from threats you can't even imagine." Shori's composure cracked. "Every difficult decision serves the greater good. Every sacrifice ensures that millions of others don't have to suffer."

"Speaking of threats you're ignoring," Nessa said, her tone shifting to something more tactical, "your security reports show increasing coordination among frontier groups. That crew that hit your eastern corridor transport last spring? They're getting bolder. And they're not alone."

"Petty criminals playing at rebellion." Shori waved dismissively. "I have bigger concerns than frontier thieves and their delusions of significance."

"You keep saying that. And they keep not being petty."

"Whose greater good? And who decided you get to make those sacrifices on everyone else's behalf?"

They stared at each other across the table, years of shared history and growing opposition crystallizing into open conflict. The careful pretense of diplomatic dinner had dissolved into something more honest and infinitely more dangerous.

"You're naive if you think the alternatives are better," Shori said finally. "Without structure, without guidance, without the kind of comprehensive planning you find so morally objectionable, this continent would tear itself apart within a generation."

"Maybe. But that would be their choice, not yours."

"Choice is a luxury that requires stability to exist. I provide that stability."

"You provide control. There's a difference."

Nessa stood with fluid precision, neither hurrying nor hesitating. "Thank you for dinner, Chief Minister. The conversation was... clarifying."

"Nessa." Shori rose from her chair. "This doesn't have to be adversarial. We can find common ground."

Nessa paused at the elevator controls, looking back with an expression that mixed sadness with determination. "We had common ground once. You chose to burn it for the sake of your larger patterns."

"I chose to preserve what matters instead of sacrificing it to sentiment."

"You helped me once when I was broken," Shori said, her voice growing quieter, more vulnerable. "You sat by my bedside and told me that failure wasn't permanent, that setbacks were just obstacles to overcome. You believed in me when I couldn't believe in myself. Why can't you trust me now when everything we worked for is finally within reach?"

Nessa's expression softened for just a moment, pain flickering across her features. "Those young women we both remember are long gone, Shori. They never entered this room. What's standing here now..." She paused, her voice becoming infinitely sad. "What's standing here now is what we became instead of who we were meant to be."

"I became what I had to become to protect what mattered most." Shori's voice cracked slightly. "Do you think I wanted this? Do you think I enjoyed watching you look at me like I was becoming a stranger? I broke us because the higher I climbed, the more dangerous loving me became for you. My enemies would have used you against me. My allies would have seen you as a weakness to exploit."

"So you made the choice for both of us."

"I made the choice that kept you alive and gave you the freedom to choose your own path. Even if that path led away from me." Shori's silver-gray eyes glistened. "Even if it meant you'd eventually stand in rooms like this, looking at me like I'm the enemy."

"No," Nessa said quietly, her hand still on the elevator controls. "You chose to become the kind of person who can't tell the difference between protection and control. Between love and possession. Between what you want to preserve and what you're actually destroying."

The elevator doors closed with a soft whisper, leaving Shori alone with the remnants of a meal that had become an interrogation.

She stood motionless for several moments. Then she reached for her wine glass with carefully controlled movements and felt it shatter in her grip.

Blood welled from a cut across her palm, dripping onto the white tablecloth in bright red drops. She grabbed a napkin, pressing it against the wound.

"Chief Minister?" A server appeared from the kitchen area. "Are you..."

"Get out." The words came out sharp, controlled but barely. "Now."

The young man retreated quickly, leaving her alone with the evidence of her momentary loss of control.

She moved to the communication terminal, pressing the napkin against her bleeding palm.

"Chief Minister?"

"The dinner is concluded. I need a comprehensive security review initiated immediately. All ministerial-level personnel. All communication networks above standard oversight." She watched blood seep through linen. "And I want a detailed analysis of Minister Kaine's activities. Every query, every access, every piece of information she's touched."

"Timeline?"

"Twelve hours."

The connection terminated. She stood alone with the city lights and the growing certainty that tomorrow would require decisive action she'd hoped to avoid.

She'd given Nessa every opportunity to step back. The dinner had been one final attempt to preserve what they'd once meant to each other while protecting what she'd built.

Nessa had chosen her path. Now she would live with the consequences.

PART FIVE

THE LEAK

Early Autumn, 2191

Hamilton Tower Residence, CAD Hamilton

The security review Shori had ordered after the dinner took twelve hours. The implications took longer.

She sat in her private residence, hardwood floors warm beneath her bare feet, wine untouched on the side table, and watched the data populate her terminal screen while Minerva watched her from the elaborate perch system near the eastern windows.

"I know," Shori murmured to the falcon. "I should have done this sooner."

Minerva's pink-glowing eyes tracked her with the unsettling intelligence that had always made the bird feel less like a companion and more like a conscience. Three feet tall and utterly dignified, she was perhaps the only living creature who could make Shori feel genuinely observed.

Elan's security review had been thorough. Nessa's access patterns across six months of Internal Affairs databases, cross-referenced with operational timelines. Hundreds of entries, most routine. Personnel files, budget reconciliations, standard oversight reviews.

But as Shori scrolled through the chronological listing, patterns emerged that confirmed everything the dinner had suggested.

Transportation Authority queries timed to coincide with asset movements. Medical supply distribution reviews filed during active operations. Personnel transfer records pulled for technical specialists whose names appeared on classified project rosters.

Nothing individually suspicious. Taken together, a systematic investigation of infrastructure that supported sensitive operations.

"Let's see what you've been looking at," Shori murmured, initiating deeper correlation analysis.

The results appeared, and her analytical calm shifted into something colder. Every significant delay during recent operations corresponded to queries from Internal Affairs. Transportation problems matched exactly with reviews of cargo manifest procedures. Medical supply shortages aligned with equipment tracking audits.

She expanded the analysis, adding historical operations. The prisoner convoy operation from 2189, where specialized assets had been lost despite careful planning. Equipment failures attributed to maintenance issues and supplier problems. But the access logs told a different story: someone in Internal Affairs had initiated reviews of transportation security protocols two days before the convoy departed.

The pattern was unmistakable. Years of careful sabotage disguised as bureaucratic inefficiency.

"Clever," she said quietly. Admiration mixing with growing anger. "Very clever."

The authentication logs confirmed what she already knew. V. Kaine, Internal Affairs. Precisely targeted. Timed with operational phases. Designed to create maximum disruption while maintaining plausible deniability.

The kind of sabotage that could only come from someone who had helped plan those operations.

Shori leaned back. The room went silent except for the distant hum of the building's systems and Minerva's soft breathing.

Nessa. My Nessa.

The realization didn't hit like a blow. It settled like weight. She'd known since the dinner. Had probably known since the corridor exchange in Late Winter, when the song changed. But knowing and seeing the proof were different things, the way knowing someone is dead and seeing the body are different things.

She sat with it. Watched the data populate. Let the analytical mind do what it did while the rest of her processed the specific devastation of watching someone she'd loved methodically destroy everything they'd built together.

A single tear traced down her cheek before she could stop it. She wiped it away with careful precision.

"That girl," she said to Minerva, who tilted her head with what might have been interest. "I helped get her where she is. The skills, the position, the access. All of it traces back to my guidance."

Minerva remained silent. Pink eyes glowing in the subdued lighting.

"Some prices are worth paying," Shori said quietly. "Even when they cost everything."

A soft chime. Elan arriving with classified documentation that confirmed what the data analysis had shown: active coordination between Internal Affairs and external networks. Intelligence sharing. Operations designed to compromise ongoing missions.

"The situation requires immediate response measures," Elan said, his voice carrying no inflection while something in his stillness suggested deeper currents.

"Recommendations?"

"Immediate containment. Communication network analysis to identify the full scope of compromise."

Shori nodded. The personal pain remained, channeled now into something more focused. More useful.

"Prepare detailed response options. And Elan? Arrange for enhanced monitoring of the Council chambers. I want to know what Minister Kaine is planning before she plans it."

"Understood completely, Chief Minister."

Outside her windows, Hamilton continued its nightly routines. Inside, Shori planned for a future where the woman she'd once loved would receive the response her betrayal demanded.

✦

Six Weeks Later | Early Autumn, 2191 Valdris Promontory

The morning sun streamed through the Council Chamber's floor-to-ceiling windows, painting the Valdris Sea in shades of gold and amber. Shori took her customary walk down the central aisle, but today she moved with particular purpose, her silver-gray eyes scanning the chamber until they found their target.

Minister Kaine sat in her usual position, fourth seat from the left, reviewing documents with what appeared to be intense focus. But something in her posture, the slight tension in her shoulders, the way she held her materials, suggested this wouldn't be routine.

Shori approached, her voice pitched for Nessa's ears alone. "Our conversation ended prematurely. We should reconvene."

Nessa looked up with careful neutrality. "I believe all necessary points were adequately addressed, Chief Minister."

"Indeed they do." Nessa's tone remained neutral. "Though some collaborations leave scars that never quite heal properly."

Shori's hand moved unconsciously to the thin pale line along her left cheek, the mark that had brought them together all those years ago. "Old wounds serve as useful reminders about the cost of failure."

"Or the price of success. Depending on how you measure such things."

Before she could pursue the conversation further, Captain Jor's voice carried across the chamber: "The Chief Minister of the Continental Authority. The Honorable Shori Ashford."

Shori settled into the Seat. The chamber felt different today. Ministers seemed more attentive than usual. Aides positioned closer to their principals. An overall sense of anticipation.

The first hour proceeded normally. Budget reconciliations. Administrative appointments. Routine business. But Shori found herself watching Nessa, noting how she occasionally consulted documents that hadn't been distributed to other ministers.

When Nessa's scheduled time arrived for Internal Affairs reporting, she rose with fluid confidence, carrying a folder more substantial than usual monthly summaries. In the gallery behind her, a tall brunette woman, Victoria Colwell, leaned forward slightly.

"Chief Minister, esteemed colleagues." Nessa's voice carried professional authority but with a slight tremor. "Internal Affairs has completed preliminary review of resource allocation patterns that warrant Council attention."

"Routine oversight matters can be handled through standard administrative channels," Shori interjected. "Unless there are specific concerns requiring legislative consultation?"

"There are indeed specific concerns." Nessa opened her folder, revealing surveillance photographs. Her hands shook almost imperceptibly.

"Concerns regarding systematic diversions of public resources to operations that lack proper oversight authorization."

"Minister Kaine, preliminary reports typically go through proper review channels before Council presentation..."

"The irregularities we've identified suggest these may not be preliminary matters." Nessa's interruption was respectful but firm, her confidence building with each word. "They appear to involve facilities funded through infrastructure budgets but constructed to specifications that don't match their official descriptions."

"The Council does not recognize unauthorized presentations of unverified intelligence," Shori said, her voice carrying the authority of eight years in the Seat. Captain Jor straightened, anticipating what would come next. His hand moved instinctively toward his ceremonial position.

Nessa faltered for just a moment, glancing uncertainly toward the gallery. In that instant, Victoria rose from her seat.

"Article Seven," Victoria whispered, her voice just loud enough to carry. "Emergency presentation protocol."

"I invoke Article Seven of the Continental Charter," Nessa said quickly. "Emergency presentation of evidence regarding potential violations of legislative authority."

Jor's movement toward the gallery stopped mid-stride. Article Seven changed everything. Even Chief Ministers couldn't override emergency protocols without proper justification.

"Article Seven requires secondary confirmation of emergency status," Shori replied with calm precision. "Are you prepared to demonstrate immediate threat justification under subsection..."

Victoria's hand touched Nessa's shoulder. Brief. Supportive. "Subsection C. Systematic violations. Legislative oversight authority."

"Subsection C," Nessa corrected immediately. "Emergency Council review of evidence suggesting systematic violations of legislative oversight authority, pending formal investigation authorization."

Technically perfect. Shori felt her procedural advantage evaporate.

"The evidence consists of facility documentation, resource allocation records, and operational photographs that suggest public funds have been diverted to programs operating outside normal authorization channels."

"This is highly irregular," Minister Dacian protested, jowls quivering. "Proper channels exist for exactly these kinds of..."

"The photographs," Nessa continued, holding up aerial surveillance images, "document construction projects funded through agricultural research budgets but built with medical-grade security perimeters, specialized ventilation systems, and what can only be described as human containment infrastructure."

She spread the images across the display area. The facilities were unmistakable. Reinforced walls. Security checkpoints. Isolation wings extending from central processing areas.

"These images show taxpayer-funded facilities with detention capabilities, medical equipment designed for involuntary procedures, and transport access that bypasses normal civilian oversight."

Minister Korvyn leaned forward, his military experience evident in how he assessed the tactical layouts. Thorne's nervous energy focused into sharp attention. Even Graylen studied the photographs with growing alarm.

Victoria remained standing in the gallery. Nessa drew confidence from her presence.

"Where did these originate?" Korvyn asked.

"Legitimate Internal Affairs oversight activities. Acquired through proper investigative protocols when suspicious patterns emerged during routine budget reviews."

"Captain Jor," Shori called. "Please escort Minister Kaine from the chamber pending proper..."

"Chief Minister." Jor's voice carried unusual hesitation. Instead of moving toward Nessa, he remained frozen between duty and conscience.

"Article Seven, subsection C does grant emergency presentation rights pending Council determination."

The hesitation was devastating. For eight years, Jor had executed her orders without question. But something in the photographs, the implications of systematic deception, had given him pause.

Nessa sensed the shift. With Victoria's steady presence behind her, she took the crucial step forward.

"The facilities documented in these photographs are processing centers for human experimentation. Children, specifically. Children taken from their families and subjected to medical procedures with documented mortality rates exceeding thirty percent."

Absolute silence. Not polite quiet. Stunned stillness.

"What the frack?" Minister Korvyn slumped into his seat.

"That's exactly what it sounds like," Nessa continued, her earlier nervousness gone. "Systematic abduction and experimentation on children, funded through your approved budgets, operating under your legislative authority."

Dacian's face had gone pale. "Chief Minister, surely these allegations are..."

"Are documented with comprehensive evidence that I will present to any formal investigation this Council authorizes," Nessa finished. She looked directly at Shori. For the first time, her expression carried not just professional challenge but personal disappointment. "The question is whether this Council has the courage to investigate crimes committed under its own authority."

"I motion for emergency investigation into these allegations," Korvyn said without hesitation.

"Seconded," from Thorne.

"Seconded," from Graylen.

Shori felt the careful equilibrium of eight years shifting beneath her feet. Forty-eight hours. If she could manage this properly, she'd have forty-eight hours to prepare countermeasures, to contact allies, to ensure any investigation found exactly what she wanted it to find.

"The facilities in question serve legitimate security purposes," she said, rising from the Seat. "Purposes that require operational classification for both effectiveness and personnel protection."

"Then they should withstand appropriate legislative review," Korvyn replied firmly. "If these are legitimate security operations, proper oversight should validate rather than threaten their mission."

The vote was definitive: seven in favor of emergency investigation, four opposed, one abstention. Her authority questioned, but not the crushing defeat that would end everything.

"The motion carries," Shori announced, her voice steady. "Internal Affairs is authorized to conduct emergency review of classified operations, subject to appropriate security protocols."

She gathered her materials with the controlled precision of someone who understood that the next forty-eight hours would determine whether her life's work survived or was destroyed by the woman who had once helped build it.

The game wasn't over. It was just entering a new phase.

CHIEF MINISTER

PART SIX

THE UNRAVELING

Early Autumn, 2191

Hamilton Tower, CAD Hamilton

An unseasonable chill gripped Hamilton as gray clouds pressed against the tower windows. The forty-eight hours since the Council vote had been an education in how quickly loyalty dissolved when power shifted.

Three governors who should have returned her calls hadn't. Two department heads sent subordinates to meetings where they'd normally appear personally. The usual flow of administrative coordination had slowed to a careful trickle.

On the wall-mounted display, Continental Broadcasting ran its morning cycle with professional neutrality that somehow made everything sound worse: "Council Authorizes Emergency Investigation Into Federal

Operations... Questions Raised About Resource Allocation... Internal Affairs Conducting Comprehensive Review..."

Someone was feeding the media just enough to shape public perception without revealing specifics. Professional. Calculated. Devastating.

Shori switched off the display and made her calls. Governor Hale's aide answered with unusual formality: "The Governor is in extended sessions regarding territorial security matters." Translation: Hale was distancing himself until he knew which way the winds would blow. Minister Collins offered "deep concern about media reports" and "full confidence in proper oversight." More diplomatic non-support.

By the third call, the pattern was clear. Everyone expressing confidence in her leadership while positioning themselves to survive whatever came next.

Elan arrived with overnight intelligence. Multiple communication intercepts. Nessa and Victoria had been working through the night, coordinating with sources across multiple territories, building a comprehensive case rather than the limited review Shori had anticipated.

"How comprehensive?" she asked.

"Facility documentation from seven locations. Personnel interviews with forty-three individuals. Financial analysis spanning eighteen months." He consulted his notes. "And testimony from what intelligence suggests may be as many as twelve enhanced individuals currently in protective custody."

The scope was staggering. She'd expected limited investigation. Instead, Nessa had prepared complete exposure.

"Timeline for formal presentation?"

"Tomorrow morning. Emergency session called for 0800." A pause. "Intelligence also suggests media coordination for simultaneous public release."

Not just political defeat. Public exposure. The kind of comprehensive revelation that would make survival impossible through normal channels.

Shori moved to her window. Hamilton's morning traffic flowing through streets that would soon be discussing her legacy in very different terms. When she turned back, her expression carried the cold calculation that had sustained her through eight years.

"Elan, I need you to handle some personal arrangements. Minerva should be taken to visit my mother. She's been looking forward to seeing her. And my personal belongings from the residence should be gathered and secured. Items with sentimental value."

Elan's expression didn't change, but something shifted in his posture. Complete understanding. "Of course, Chief Minister. Shall I coordinate with our friends regarding transportation and logistics?"

"Yes. They'll want to help with such personal matters. Ensure everything is handled with appropriate discretion. Some belongings are quite valuable."

"Understood completely."

As Elan departed to implement arrangements that had nothing to do with family visits or sentimental items, Shori felt the familiar transition from public leadership to operational planning.

If tomorrow brought political destruction, she would be prepared for whatever came after.

✧

The afternoon brought a parade of careful conversations and diplomatic betrayals. But it was the conversation that didn't follow the pattern that proved most revealing.

Dr. Evelyn Baeriss arrived for their scheduled consultation with enthusiasm entirely disconnected from the political crisis surrounding them.

"The transition arrangements are proceeding smoothly," she reported, settling into her chair. "Alternative procurement networks have been established. Personnel transfers coordinated. Operational capabilities will continue without interruption."

"Alternative networks?"

"The Andori connections you suggested. Remarkably efficient once you adjust for their different organizational priorities." Evelyn consulted her notes. "Less bureaucratic oversight. More direct resource allocation. In many ways, this could prove more effective than official channels."

"Less precise methods, though."

"More crude, certainly. But more flexible. Without legislative constraints, we can accelerate timelines, expand scope, implement procedures that would require months of approval through official channels." Her eyes gleamed behind round glasses. "The work is too important to be constrained by democratic sentiment."

The casual dismissal of "democratic sentiment" as an obstacle crystallized everything. Shori recognized her own justifications reflected back through Evelyn's analytical perspective.

"Enhanced individuals in protective custody," she said. "How many compromised?"

"Twelve confirmed. But the processing records were maintained in secure systems. Whatever testimony they provide will lack supporting documentation." Evelyn waved dismissively. "Personal accounts without official verification. Politically damaging but not operationally critical."

Twelve people who had survived systematic experimentation, dismissed as a public relations problem.

Commotion from the outer office interrupted them. Raised voices. Urgent movement. Tension cutting through the usual administrative calm.

"Chief Minister!" The voice belonged to Dani Castell, but carried an edge Shori had never heard before. The young woman burst through the door without announcement, her usual bright demeanor replaced by something approaching devastation.

"Is it true?" Dani asked, tears streaming down her cheeks as she clutched a folder of documents. "The things they're saying about the facilities. About what happens to the families. About the children."

Shori felt her composure crack at the sight of genuine anguish in someone she'd genuinely cared about. Dani represented something approaching innocence in her world, enthusiastic competence unmarred by the moral complexity that defined most relationships at her level of authority.

"Dani, the situation is more complex than media reports suggest. The work we do requires..."

"Children," Dani interrupted, her voice growing stronger despite the tears. "You're taking children from their families. Processing them in secret facilities. Using them like..." She couldn't finish the sentence, but her expression completed the thought.

"I'm protecting the continent from threats that most people can't understand. Everything I do serves the greater good, even when individual elements seem difficult to accept."

"The greater good?" Dani's voice cracked with something between disbelief and heartbreak. "Chief Minister, I thought... I believed in you. I thought you were different. Better. Someone who cared about people instead of just using them."

She set a folder on Shori's desk with trembling hands. "My resignation. Effective immediately."

"Dani, you're making an emotional decision based on incomplete information. If you'd just..."

"No." The young woman wiped tears from her cheeks with angry precision. "I'm making a moral decision based on who I am versus who I thought you were."

She moved toward the door, then paused to look back.

"I hope it was worth it," she said quietly. "Whatever you think you're protecting, I hope it was worth becoming the kind of person who can justify this."

The door closed behind her with devastating finality.

"Unfortunate," Evelyn observed with clinical detachment. "Though predictable. Emotional attachment to abstract principles rather than practical outcomes."

✧

An hour later, Captain Jor appeared in her office doorway with the formal bearing that had marked fifteen years of distinguished service. But something in his posture suggested this wasn't a routine security briefing.

"Chief Minister. I need to discuss my continued service with your administration."

Shori felt ice settle in her stomach. "Captain?"

Without ceremony, Jor reached into his jacket and withdrew his service pin, the symbol that had marked fifteen years of unwavering loyalty. He placed it on her desk with the careful precision of someone performing a ritual that mattered.

"I can't protect this anymore," he said, his voice steady despite the magnitude of what he was doing. "I can't stand guard while children are processed like materials. I can't maintain protocols that serve this kind of operation."

The pin lay on the polished wood like an accusation. For a moment, the office was completely silent except for the distant hum of building systems.

"Captain, you're making a serious mistake. Walking away from your duty, abandoning your responsibilities, betraying the trust that's been placed in you."

"I'm honoring the duty I swore to uphold," Jor replied, his gaze direct despite the pain in his expression. "Protecting people. Serving justice. Maintaining the principles this government was founded to defend." He paused. "I can't do that while protecting operations that violate everything I believed we stood for."

He turned toward the door with military precision, then paused at the threshold.

"Chief Minister, I hope someday you remember who you used to be before you became this."

The door closed with a soft click.

✧

Evening found Shori in her private residence, seeking familiar comfort after a day that had stripped away illusions about loyalty. But even here, sanctuary had been violated.

The space had been searched. Not ransacked, but professionally examined with surgical precision. Drawers closed but misaligned. Documents restacked in different order. Personal items repositioned just enough to signal thorough examination.

"Your falcon," Evelyn observed, noting the empty perch system. "Where is she?"

"Safe," Shori replied, though the silence in her residence felt heavier without Minerva's presence. For the first time in years, her most loyal companion was elsewhere, as if even the falcon had sensed what was coming.

They stood in the violated space, surrounded by evidence that Nessa's investigation had extended far beyond official facilities. Private communications, personal files, intimate correspondence, all of it examined, catalogued, probably copied for tomorrow's presentation.

"How much do they know?" Shori asked.

"Everything," Evelyn replied. "Financial records, operational details, personnel files, communication logs. Every document that could support a comprehensive case."

"And you're not concerned?"

"Why would I be? The work continues regardless of political complications." Evelyn's smile carried cold satisfaction. "They can investigate and regulate and oversee all they want. The real work is beyond their bureaucratic reach."

A soft chime from her secure terminal. Shori turned to the amber-brown monitor, its green phosphor text materializing line by line:

PRIORITY SECURE / EYES ONLY

FROM: Agent A. Revalis
TO: Chief Minister S. Ashford
RE: Southeastern Assessment

Extraction complete. Asset secured. Subject 512-D en route to processing facility via alternative network. No complications. Local resistance minimal. Baseline measurements exceed standard thresholds by factor of 1.7. Secondary materials acquired as specified.

Agent Revalis

She read the message twice. While her authority faced systematic challenge and personal loyalties dissolved around her, Aerin had delivered exactly what the program required: another candidate, cleanly extracted and ready for processing.

"Success?" Evelyn asked.

"Complete success. Subject 512-D is secure and en route."

"Excellent. See? The real work continues regardless of political theater." Evelyn gathered her materials. "I'll coordinate transition protocols with our alternative networks."

As Evelyn departed, Shori stood alone in her violated residence, watching Hamilton's lights spread toward the horizon through windows that no longer felt secure. Tomorrow would bring the end of her official authority. But it would also bring liberation from the constraints that had limited her for eight years.

They could destroy her political career. They couldn't stop the work.

Tomorrow would bring the end of Chief Minister Shori Ashford. But it would also bring the beginning of something more honest about what power actually meant, and what protecting civilization actually cost.

CHIEF MINISTER

PART SEVEN

MOTION CARRIED

Late Autumn, 2191
Valdris Promontory, CAD Hamilton

— ❖ —

Shori Ashford returned to the Valdris Promontory, making her way through the marble corridors toward the 0800 emergency session, what Internal Affairs had described as an "urgent presentation of critical findings," and noticed immediately that everything fundamental had changed.

Staff members who would normally approach for brief consultations now found sudden interest in documents, doorways, anything that allowed them to avoid direct interaction. Conversations died mid-sentence as she passed. Even her security detail felt different. New faces, unfamiliar bearing, the rigid protocol of personnel following orders rather than serving from loyalty.

Captain Jor was gone. In his place, Captain Reese maintained professional distance with the kind of formality that spoke of institutional duty rather than personal commitment.

But Shori had spent the past twenty-four hours processing Elan's intelligence reports. Twelve enhanced individuals in protective custody. Comprehensive facility documentation. Financial analysis spanning eighteen months. The scope was staggering, but she'd prepared for this possibility. Her extraction protocols were in place. Her allies were positioned. Whatever political theater unfolded here, her work would continue.

She entered the Council Chamber with the same measured pace that had commanded respect for eight years. But the familiar rhythms felt different now. Charged with the kind of anticipation that preceded either triumph or execution.

Where ministers would normally rise in acknowledgment, several remained seated. Where aides would typically maintain respectful attention, many avoided eye contact entirely. The gallery seemed more crowded than usual, filled with staff whose expressions suggested they expected to witness something historic.

But it was the figure waiting at the outskirts of the central presentation area that commanded attention. Victoria Colwell stood with the bearing of someone who had spent eight years preparing for this moment, her dark hair perfectly arranged, her reading glasses catching the light as she organized materials with practiced efficiency. This wasn't Pence's quiet aide anymore. This was someone who had found her true arena.

Beside her, Nessa appeared unusually formal despite being the official presenter. She carried herself with obvious tension, but when she looked at Victoria, her expression carried gratitude for someone who had made this moment possible.

"The Chief Minister of the Continental Authority," announced Captain Reese with mechanical precision. "The Honorable Shori Ashford."

Shori reached the Seat and remained standing. Some met her gaze with familiar respect. Others studied their materials with uncomfortable intensity. All of them were here. All of them were listening.

"Ministers. I understand Internal Affairs has requested this emergency session to present findings from their recent investigation. I look forward to addressing any concerns and providing proper context for complex security operations that require careful explanation."

"Please be seated."

As she completed the ceremonial opening, Nessa stepped forward.

"Chief Minister, esteemed ministers. What you are about to hear represents the most comprehensive investigation in the history of Internal Affairs. An investigation that has uncovered systematic violations of legislative authority, constitutional principles, and basic human rights."

The chamber fell silent.

"However, given the complex procedural requirements and the sheer scope of evidence, I'm turning this presentation over to someone with unparalleled expertise in legislative oversight and governmental accountability." She stepped aside. "Victoria Colwell."

A murmur rippled through the chamber. Many recognized Victoria's name from her years with Pence Garda. In the gallery, aides leaned forward.

Victoria stepped forward with confident authority that made the chamber's energy shift. Her bearing was that of someone who had mastered every procedural detail of continental governance and spent eight years preparing for exactly this moment.

"Thank you, Minister Kaine. Ministers, what I will present today is not merely an investigation report. It is comprehensive documentation of thirty-eight years of systematic crimes committed under the authority of this Council, funded through your approved budgets, and conducted in facilities bearing your legislative authorization."

She activated the projection system, displaying an organizational chart that made several ministers lean forward with alarm. The complete structure of what she labeled "The Ossuary Program": facility locations, personnel hierarchies, operational timelines, budget allocations connecting directly to legislation they had approved.

"The Continental Genetic Wellness Initiative was approved by this Council in 2153 with a mandate to study inherited medical conditions. Under Dr. Efram Odell, it began as legitimate research into ferric blood anomaly, a rare condition that provided natural immunity to the Rose Fever. Dr. Odell's vaccine eliminated Rose Fever as a continental threat and saved thousands of lives. However, what began as medical research evolved into something far more sinister."

She advanced to the timeline of transformation. "By 2150, the facility had established what they called 'The Ossuary,' a classified sublevel dedicated to 'specialized research' focused on individuals with elevated ferric markers in their blood."

Victoria walked the Council through the systematic evolution from legitimate research to human experimentation, showing how each authorization they'd approved had been used to expand capabilities for human modification.

"The program that you have unknowingly, some perhaps knowingly, funded all these years has operated as a systematic program of child abduction and human experimentation."

Minister Korvyn's face went pale. "These facility locations... some of these were presented to us as agricultural research stations."

"Exactly. What you approved as 'genetic research laboratories' were constructed as processing centers designed for human subject containment, involuntary medical procedures, and systematic human modification."

The architectural plans were devastating in their detail. Containment cells disguised as medical suites. Processing areas equipped for sustained procedures on unwilling subjects. Transport access designed to bypass civilian oversight.

"The scope includes seventeen active facilities across nine territories, with documented processing of two hundred and thirty-seven subjects over the past five years alone."

"Two hundred children," Minister Thorne said quietly.

"Two hundred and thirty-seven confirmed cases," Victoria corrected. "Current facilities maintain capacity for simultaneous processing of up to seventy-five individuals, with projected expansion plans that would have tripled that capacity within eighteen months."

She gestured to Nessa, who stepped forward with a folder thick enough to suggest comprehensive documentation.

"Minister Kaine will now present testimony from twelve enhanced individuals currently in protective custody. Survivors who can provide firsthand accounts of procedures conducted in these facilities."

Nessa opened her folder. "These testimonies describe systematic programs designed not to study genetic conditions, but to create them. To modify human physiology through procedures with documented mortality rates exceeding thirty percent."

She read excerpts. Children taken from families under false pretenses. Medical procedures designed to enhance physical capabilities. Systems that treated them as raw materials rather than human beings.

"Subject 187-C, female, age fourteen at time of processing. Eighteen months of involuntary medical procedures. Surgical implantation of foreign materials. Repeated exposure to experimental compounds. Psychological conditioning designed to eliminate emotional responses incompatible with operational efficiency."

The chamber had gone silent except for the sound of pages turning.

"Subject 201-A, male, age sixteen at processing. Family told he had been selected for advanced educational opportunities. Twenty-six months of procedures designed to enhance sensory capabilities. Systematic psychological manipulation designed to transfer emotional loyalty from family to institutional authority."

"What the fuck?" Minister Korvyn slumped into his seat.

"What the fuck, indeed?" Victoria stepped forward, reclaiming control. "The testimonies are supported by comprehensive documentary evidence." She activated new projections: medical records, procedural logs, authorization chains connecting every operation to specific officials and approved budgets.

"Financial analysis reveals that over the past five years, this Council has unknowingly authorized 847 million holdings for facilities and programs described as agricultural research, genetic wellness initiatives, and territorial development projects. Those funds were systematically diverted to support human experimentation on an industrial scale."

"The authorization chains show direct oversight responsibility extending to the highest levels of continental authority as recently as this administration. Chief Minister Ashford has maintained direct operational oversight of the Ossuary Program since her appointment to office. Including personal authorization of specific extraction operations, facility expansions, and procedural modifications designed to increase both capacity and efficiency."

Minister Dacian's jowls quivered. "Chief Minister, these documents suggest we've been funding systematic torture of children."

Victoria stepped forward again, her command of the chamber absolute.

"The evidence includes operational reports from as recently as this week. Including authorization for ongoing extraction operations that continued even after this investigation was announced."

The projection showed message logs from Agent Revalis reporting successful completion of an extraction: Subject 512-D, southeastern assessment, asset secured and en route to processing facility via alternative network.

"Even while this Council was authorizing investigation into these programs," Victoria said, "Chief Minister Ashford was continuing to authorize new victims."

Absolute silence. Not political shock. Moral devastation.

"I move for immediate suspension of executive authority over all classified operations," Korvyn said.

"Seconded," came from multiple voices.

Victoria consulted procedural documents. "Under Article Twelve of the Continental Charter, emergency suspension of executive authority requires a two-thirds majority vote of the full Council. However, given the scope of criminal activity documented here, I recommend the Council also consider Article Fifteen: immediate transfer of authority pending criminal investigation."

The chamber erupted in murmurs. Article Fifteen meant not just suspension. Arrest.

"All in favor of emergency suspension of Chief Minister Ashford's executive authority pending criminal investigation?"

Ten ministers in favor. One opposed. One abstention.

Victoria wasn't finished.

"Under Article Fifteen, I further move for immediate arrest pending formal criminal charges."

"Seconded," from Korvyn.

Eleven in favor. Zero opposed. One abstention.

"The motion carries," Shori announced, her voice steady despite the magnitude of the defeat. "Executive authority is suspended and transfer of custody is authorized pending comprehensive criminal investigation."

The chamber erupted. Aides rushed toward the central floor, ministers rose in confusion, urgent conversations broke out across the gallery. Never in the history of the Continental Authority had a sitting Chief Minister been arrested in chambers.

Captain Reese moved with immediate precision, producing restraints as he approached the Seat. "Chief Minister Shori Ashford, you are under arrest pending criminal investigation."

The metallic click of handcuffs echoed through the chamber like a gunshot, cutting through the chaos and making everything suddenly, devastatingly real.

"Security, clear a path," Reese commanded.

But as they began moving toward the chamber's main exit, Dani Castell broke from the gallery and rushed toward them, her composure completely abandoned.

"Shori!" she called, pushing past security personnel with surprising determination.

Before anyone could stop her, she wrapped her arms around the restrained Chief Minister in a fierce embrace, tears streaming down her cheeks.

"I'm so sorry," she whispered urgently against Shori's ear. "The resignation, the emotional display, it was all for optics. I needed them to believe I'd turned against you. I'm sorry you had to see me like that."

Shori looked down at the young woman with something approaching genuine affection, understanding flooding her expression. "Clever girl," she murmured. "You played it perfectly."

"Ma'am, we need to move," Reese said, though he allowed the moment to continue longer than protocol demanded.

As they separated, Dani fell into step beside the security detail, her presence somehow accepted without question despite the breach of protocol.

"Where are we going?" Shori asked as they resumed their procession.

"To join your friends," Reese replied with professional courtesy that somehow managed to sound reassuring rather than ominous.

The chamber doors closed behind them with finality.

✪

The secure transport bay opened to reveal vehicles that bore official markings but somehow felt different from standard government transportation. The security personnel guided both Shori and Dani with respectful efficiency toward an armored sedan.

Hamilton's ordered streets flowed past the windows. Normal traffic. Routine commerce. Citizens pursuing their lives without awareness that the continental balance of power had just shifted.

The house appeared ahead. A modest residence surrounded by well-maintained gardens, comfortable domesticity that spoke of peaceful retirement rather than operational security. But as the vehicle stopped, Shori noted details that suggested this haven was more complex than its appearance indicated.

One figure waited on the front porch: Elan Trevare with his characteristic efficiency intact, bearing suggesting satisfaction rather than concern about her legal situation.

"Chief Minister," Elan acknowledged as they approached. "Ms. Castell. Excellent performance today."

Dani managed a small smile through her lingering emotion. "Thank you. It was harder than I expected."

"The best performances always are," Shori observed. "And it is Director Ashford now."

✦

The afternoon sun painted everything in warm golden light. The gardens. The house. Elan waiting with his characteristic efficiency. Dani beside her, composure returning.

And Minerva. Descending with regal grace to land on the portable perch Elan had positioned with obvious care. Emerald and gold plumage catching the light. Pink-glowing eyes that shifted between warmth and judgment.

"There you are," Shori said softly, approaching to stroke the falcon's feathers. "I was wondering when you'd return."

The domestic scene settled around her. Former Chief Minister. Loyal staff. Magnificent companion. Comfortable retirement. The kind of resolution that allowed everyone to feel justice had been served.

Shori's hand moved along Minerva's plumage, her voice dropping to the register she used only when masks were unnecessary.

"They think they destroyed me," she murmured. The falcon's pink eyes tracked her face with unsettling intelligence. "They've given me exactly what I needed. Freedom to do what's necessary without the burden of explaining it to people who lack the vision to understand."

Her fingers paused on the falcon's neck.

"You want to know why I didn't drag Nessa down with me? Why I didn't expose her trafficking work with the Andori? Her recruitment of assets? Her participation in the very operations she now condemns?"

Minerva tilted her head. Shori smiled. No warmth in it.

"Because I loved her once. Because she was the one person who knew me before I became this." She resumed stroking. "And because I needed her to believe she was fighting a monster. Not becoming one herself."

She looked out at the garden, the ordered light, the careful architecture of a safe house disguised as retirement.

"She was always meant to be the hero of this story. I just provided the monster for her to fight."

The falcon blinked. Shori's hand stilled.

"The beautiful irony is that every method she used against me, every network she built, every asset she recruited and shaped and broke... she learned from me. The student became the teacher. And neither of us noticed when the lesson changed from opposition to replication."

Elan appeared at the doorway. "Director Ashford. Your communications are prepared."

"Director." She tested the word. It fit differently than Chief Minister. Lighter. Less constrained.

"Coming," she said. One final stroke along Minerva's plumage. The falcon's pink eyes held hers.

"The real work continues," Shori told the bird. "It always does."

NESSA CODA

The Night Before

Early Autumn, 2191
Minister of Internal Affairs, CAD Hamilton

— ❖ —

The night before we destroyed her, I sat in my office and tried to remember who I used to be.

Victoria arrived first. Rhowan twenty minutes later, travel dust still on his coat, portfolio under his arm. The Stonewake Group's intelligence network had been running at capacity for weeks, feeding us information that Victoria had been translating into parliamentary ammunition since the investigation began.

"Ah, the prodigal consultant." Victoria didn't look up from her timeline notes. "I was beginning to think you'd gotten lost between territories."

Rhowan's mouth curved into that characteristic smile. "I'm flattered you noticed my absence."

"Had I known I'd end up working with criminals and killers, I might've gotten a tetanus booster."

"I'm flattered you think I'm dangerous enough to require medical precautions."

"Please. I remember our get-together last month and you still hadn't got the nerve to ask that copper-headed girl out."

I sighed. If I didn't put a stop to this now, they would keep at it for hours. "Children. Focus."

"Of course," Rhowan said, moving further into the room, setting his portfolio on the table. "Though I should mention that Stonewake Group maintains excellent health and safety standards."

Victoria studied him with the analytical gaze she'd perfected during eight years of managing political personalities. "Stonewake Group. I've heard whispers about that particular consulting firm."

"All good things, I hope."

"Cross-border intelligence brokerage," I translated, opening his portfolio to reveal communication intercepts, financial records, and surveillance reports. "Rhowan's been tracking Shori's extraction networks for the past six months. And he has a hard time keeping confidential information confidential."

"Guilty as charged." That smile. "Discretion was always a skill I failed to learn properly, but I do know how to read a room."

"Do you?" Victoria asked dryly.

Victoria leaned forward, attention shifting to the documents. The papers Rhowan had brought weren't just intelligence. They were comprehensive documentation of escape routes, safe houses, and resource caches spanning multiple territories.

"These communication logs show coordination with assets outside Continental Authority jurisdiction," Victoria said. "Andori connections.

Financial transfers, identity documentation, transportation arrangements. Everything she'd need for a clean disappearance."

"Timeline?" Victoria asked.

"She's been building these networks for years," Rhowan said. "But recent activity suggests activation protocols are already in place. The moment she feels genuinely threatened, she can be beyond our reach within twenty-four hours."

"Which brings us to tomorrow," I said. "Your intelligence changes our parliamentary strategy. We're not just presenting evidence. We're closing off her escape routes."

"Exactly." Rhowan gathered his materials. "Though I should mention that forcing someone like Shori into a corner tends to make them more dangerous, not less."

"We've accounted for that possibility," I said quietly, knowing what I had to do next.

"I should go," Rhowan said, rising. "Travel arrangements to make, communication protocols to establish."

"Rhowan." I called him at the door. "Thank you. For the intelligence, for the risk, for understanding what needed to be done."

He paused at the threshold. That smile softened into something more genuine. "Some fights choose you, Nessa. This one chose all of us."

The door closed behind him. Victoria and I alone with intelligence that had just transformed tomorrow's session from political theater into something approaching justice.

⚙

"Why don't you take control tomorrow?"

Victoria blinked. "Me? Why on Tanith is that a good idea?"

"Because you have a bite that chamber forgets, Victoria. They see Pence's quiet aide, the woman who brings coffee and manages schedules. They don't see someone who knows every rule, every precedent, every procedural trap better than they do." I leaned back. "I'm dangerous in my environment. Give me a rifle and rough terrain, and I can handle any threat. But in that chamber? You're infinitely more lethal than I could ever be."

Victoria's professional mask slipped, revealing something that looked like nervous excitement. "It would be... satisfying to remind them that underestimating administrative staff is a career-limiting mistake."

"And you'd be magnificent at it."

She straightened. For a moment I caught a glimpse of the predator beneath the administrative efficiency. "I have been looking forward to using some of the more obscure provisions I've memorized over the years."

Then her composure cracked, just for a moment.

"This isn't just about justice for the enhanced individuals," Victoria said quietly, her voice carrying an edge I'd never heard before. "This is about what she did to Pence. What she did to Jaden. What she would have done to his entire family if we hadn't..."

She stopped. Drew a careful breath.

"Eight years, Nessa. Eight years I've been building toward this moment. Eight years of watching her hold the power she stole through systematic terrorism against a good man who loved her like family."

The pain in her voice caught me off guard. I'd seen Victoria as the perfect political weapon. But this was personal in a way that made her infinitely more dangerous.

"She forced his resignation by threatening children. Elderly relatives. Anyone he cared about." Victoria's hands trembled as she organized her materials. Eight years of controlled fury finally finding expression. "He died believing he'd failed. Believing that his life's work meant nothing because he couldn't stop her from taking power."

I understood then why Victoria had been so methodical, so patient, so devastatingly thorough. This wasn't political opposition. This was someone who had spent eight years planning to destroy the person who destroyed the only family she'd ever known.

"Thank you, Vicky," I said. "For all of this."

She paused. Looked up with an expression that had shifted completely from professional courtesy toward something genuine and warm, with steel underneath.

"You are most welcome, Nessa."

The use of my first name. After months of working together, of building trust and strategy, she had finally stopped seeing me as Minister Kaine.

✦

After Victoria left to prepare, I sat in the quiet and tried to figure out what came next.

Not tomorrow. Tomorrow was Victoria's arena. She would be magnificent and devastating and everything the chamber didn't expect.

After.

Shori wouldn't submit to arrest. She'd activate extraction procedures she'd spent years preparing. Safe houses, false identities, resources beyond official oversight. The moment she realized what was happening, she became infinitely more dangerous than she'd ever been as Chief Minister. Because she'd no longer be constrained by political considerations.

I opened the secure drawer.

I'd been telling myself this was about stopping the enhanced individual program. About justice for the victims. About preventing future atrocities. All true. All necessary.

Also not the whole truth.

I pulled out paper and started writing by hand. Electronic communications left traces. This message needed to stay invisible.

Find Regal.

There. His name on paper. No taking it back.

The woman who destroyed your family is about to disappear. Six days, maybe less. I'm giving you what I should have given you years ago. Her routes, her safe houses, her new identity.

Everything you need is enclosed.

I tried to protect her from you once. I won't make that mistake again.

I sealed the letter and wrote "S. Calder" on the outside. Snips would find Regal. Regal would understand what to do with the information.

I stared at the sealed envelope. My own words in my own handwriting.

The realization hit like a physical blow.

I sank back into my chair. The pattern was so obvious now. How had I been blind to it for so long?

Regal. Young, desperate, carrying his broken sister through a frozen wasteland. I'd found him at his most vulnerable and offered him exactly what his trauma demanded: purpose, training, a target for his rage. I'd shaped his guilt into loyalty. I'd taken his need for justice and molded it into a weapon pointed at my enemies.

Just like Shori had done with Elan. Just like Shori had done with Aerin.

Sometimes the most broken tools are the most useful ones.

My own words. Spoken to Regal about Snips, years ago. Casual. Clinical. The exact tone Shori might have used about any of her enhanced individuals.

I thought about Snips. Anne Calder. Found her already shattered. And what had I done? Refined the breaks. Made them useful. Shaped her trauma into loyalty, her pain into precision, her humanity into a tool that served my purposes.

Victoria. Brilliant, competent Victoria who'd lost someone she loved. I'd recruited her by offering what she wanted most: revenge disguised as justice. I'd shaped her institutional knowledge, her procedural expertise, her need for vindication into the perfect weapon.

And she was grateful. They were all grateful. Just like Elan was grateful to Shori.

Find broken people. Offer them purpose. Shape their pain into usefulness. Deploy them against targets. Always for the greater good.

Shori took children and turned them into enhanced soldiers. I took traumatized adults and turned them into network assets. The methodology was identical.

I pulled out fresh paper and wrote three words.

I became her.

I read them again. And again.

Each time the words did the same thing to me. The truth doesn't shift on the third read when you've stopped lying on the first.

The handoff happened in a place that technically didn't exist. Five minutes. Envelope for payment. Confirmation of timeline. Then the courier melted back into the crowd.

Walking back through Hamilton's streets, I felt the full weight of what I'd just set in motion. Tomorrow we'd destroy Shori's political career. Tonight I'd potentially signed her death warrant.

My former student sent to hunt my former lover. The weapon I built aimed at the woman who taught me to build weapons.

Back in my office, I sat in the chair Victoria had vacated and stared at the city lights until they blurred.

When had I started crying?

The children deserved better. Homes. Families. Normal lives instead of laboratories. Someone had to speak for them, and somehow that burden had fallen to me. The whole atrocity needed to end.

That didn't make this feel any less like the ultimate betrayal of everything we'd once meant to each other.

I wiped my eyes. Looked at the three words on the fresh paper, still sitting on my desk.

I became her.

Tomorrow would bring the fall of Chief Minister Shori Ashford.

I loaded the gun and aimed it at the target. Now it was time for someone else to pull the trigger.

ABOUT THE AUTHOR

JT Baldwin spent thirty years carrying the world of Blood & Steel before he ever wrote it down. The first sketches lived in notebooks shared with his twin brother — game designs, comic characters, half-built mythologies that never quite let him go. They matured in silence through a career that took him from military service to long-haul trucking across the country, the kind of work that leaves a person alone with their thoughts for ten hours at a time. The characters traveled with him.

The Blood & Steel saga foundation is built on three interlocking series: the Ironforged novels, beginning with *Wilted Crowns*; *The Palisade Journals*, a five-novella collection charting the decades of conspiracy and resistance that shape everything to come; and *Forged in Blood & Steel*, an ongoing collection of short stories from the world. He believes the best stories leave readers with something worth thinking about long after the last page — and that the second read should be richer than the first.

He lives in southeastern Minnesota with his wife, where the world keeps growing and the winters are too damn cold and long.

www.ingramcontent.com/pod-product-compliance
Lightning Source LLC
Chambersburg PA
CBHW022044170626
46808CB00003B/1355